Nursery Rhymes

illustrated by Sandy Nightingale

© The Medici Society Ltd., London, 1978.   Printed in England.   SBN 85503 048 8

Boys and girls, come out to play,
The moon doth shine as bright as day;

Come with a whoop, and come with a call,
Come with good will or come not at all.

Leave your supper and leave your sleep,
Come with your playfellows into the street.

Up the ladder and down the wall,
A halfpenny loaf will serve us all;

You find milk, and I'll find flour,
And we'll have a pudding in half an hour.

Little boy blue, come, blow up your horn;
The sheep's in the meadow, the cow's in the corn.
Where's the little boy that looks after the sheep?
Under the haystack, fast asleep.

Little Boy Blue

3

Little Bo-Peep has lost her sheep,
　　And can't tell where to find them;
Leave them alone, and they'll come home,
　　And bring their tails behind them.

Little Bo-Peep fell fast asleep,
　　And dreamt she heard them bleating;
But when she awoke she found it a joke,
　　For they were still a-fleeting.

Then up she took her little crook,
　　Determined for to find them;
She found them indeed, but it made her heart blee
　　For they'd left their tails behind them.

It happened one day as Bo-Peep did stray
　　Into a meadow hard by,
There she espied their tails side by side,
　　All hung on a tree to dry.

She heaved a sigh and wiped her eye,
　　And went over hill and dale, oh!
And tried what she could, as a shepherdess should,
　　To tack to each sheep its tail, oh!

Little Jack Horner,
　　Sat in a corner,
Eating a Christmas pie;
　　He put in his thumb,
And pulled out a plum,
　　And said, 'What a good boy am I.'

Little Bo-Peep

Mary had a little lamb
Whose fleece was white as snow,
And everywhere that Mary went
That lamb was sure to go.

It followed her to school one day
Which was against the rule.
It made the children laugh and play
To see a lamb at school.

And so the teacher turned it out,
But still it lingered near,
And waited patiently about
Till Mary did appear.

'What makes the lamb love Mary so?'
The eager children cry,
'Why, Mary loves the lamb, you know!'
The teacher did reply.

To market, to market,
To buy a fat pig;
Home again, home again,
Jiggety jig.

To market, to market,
To buy a fat hog;
Home again, home again,
Jiggety jog.

6

Mary had a little lamb

There was an old woman tossed up in a basket
Seventeen times as high as the moon;
Where she was going I couldn't but ask it,
For in her hand she carried a broom.

'Old woman, old woman, old woman,' quoth I,
'Where are you going to up so high?'
'To brush the cobwebs off the sky!'
'May I go with thee?' 'Aye, by-and-by.'

Twinkle, twinkle, little star,
How I wonder what you are!
Up above the world so high
Like a diamond in the sky.

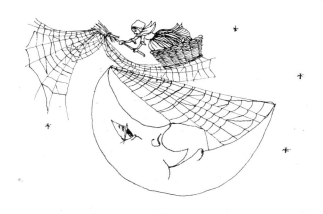

Ride a cock-horse
To Banbury Cross,
To see a fine Lady
Upon a white horse.

With rings on her fingers
And bells on her toes,
She shall have music
Wherever she goes.

There was an old woman
        who lived in a shoe;
She had so many children
        she didn't know what to do;
She gave them some broth
        without any bread;
She whipped them all soundly
        and put them to bed.

Ride a cock-horse

A counting rhyme

5 6
pick
up
sticks

1 2
buckle
my
shoe

7 8
lay
them
straight

3 4
knock
at the
door

9 10
a big
fat
hen

11
12
dig
and
delve

17
18
maids
in
waiting

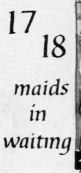

13
14
maids
a-
courting

19
20
my
plate's
empty

5
16
maids
in the
kitchen

Hush-a-bye, baby,
On the tree top;
When the wind blows,
The cradle will rock;
When the bough breaks,
The cradle will fall;
Down will come baby,
Cradle and all.

See, saw, Margery Daw,
Johnny shall have a new master;
He shall have but a penny a day,
Because he can't work any faster.

Humpty Dumpty sat on a wall,
Humpty Dumpty had a great fall;
All the king's horses and all the king's men
Couldn't put Humpty together again.

Little Miss Muffet
Sat on a tuffet,
Eating her curds and whey;
There came a great spider,
And sat down beside her,
And frightened Miss Muffet away.

Rub-a-dub-dub,
Three men in a tub;
And who do you think they be?

The butcher, the baker,
The candlestick-maker;
Turn 'em out, knaves all three!

Hey! diddle, diddle,
   The cat and the fiddle,
The cow jumped over the moon;
   The little dog laughed
   To see such sport,
And the dish ran away with the spoon.

Baa, baa, black sheep,
　　Have you any wool?
'Yes, sir, yes, sir,
　　Three bags full:
One for my master,
　　And one for my dame,
And one for the little boy
　　Who lives down the lane.'

Diddle, diddle, dumpling, my son John
Went to bed with his trousers on;
One shoe off, and one shoe on,
Diddle, diddle, dumpling, my son John.

Wee Willie Winkie runs through the town,
Up stairs and down stairs, in his nightgown,
Rapping at the window,
             crying through the lock:
'Are the children in their beds?
             —for it's past eight o'clock!'

Jack and Jill went up the hill
    To fetch a pail of water;
Jack fell down and broke his crown,
    And Jill came tumbling after.

Then up Jack got and home did trot
    As fast as he could caper;
And went to bed to mend his head
    With vinegar and brown paper.

Wee Willie Winkie

Early to bed, and early to rise,
Makes a man healthy, wealthy, and wise.